Felix the Fluffy Kitten

"Oh, they're all lovely!" Jodie said, as five tiny kittens played about her feet. There were three fluffy grey kittens, like their mum, and two sweet black and white ones with pink noses.

Jodie sighed deeply. "I'm *never* going to be able to choose!"

Hannah J

Titles in Jenny Dale's KITTEN TALES™ series

All of Jenny Dale's KITTEN TALES books can be ordered at your local bookshop or are available by post from Book Service by Post (tel: 01624 675137)

Felix the Fluffy Kitten

by Jenny Dale

Illustrated by Susan Hellard

A Working Partners Book

MACMILLAN CHILDREN'S BOOKS

To Daisy – another fluffy kitten

Special thanks to Mary Hooper

First published 1999 by Macmillan Children's Books
a division of Pan Macmillan Limited
20 New Wharf Road, London N1 9RR
Basingstoke and Oxford
www.panmacmillan.com

Associated companies throughout the world

Created by Working Partners Limited, London W6 0QT

ISBN 0 330 37453 2

7 9 8

A CIP catalogue record for this book is available from
the British Library.

Typeset by SX Composing DTP, Rayleigh, Essex
Printed and bound in Great Britain by Mackays of Chatham plc, Kent

Chapter One

Jodie Taylor woke with a start
and remembered what day it was.
She jumped out of bed and ran
straight downstairs in her
pyjamas.

"Happy birthday, sleepy head!"
her mum said as Jodie bounced
into the kitchen. "I was just about

to come and wake you up. Fancy sleeping in late today!"

"I was awake at five o'clock, wondering what presents I'd get," Jodie said, rubbing her eyes. "But then I snoozed off again."

Jodie's dad came into the kitchen with his coat on. "Happy birthday, love!" He looked at his watch. "I'll just about have time to watch you open your presents."

Jodie looked excitedly at the pile of cards and presents beside her cereal bowl. She sat down and began opening them.

There was a soft pink sweater from her nana, a computer game from Uncle Jack and a rucksack in the shape of a lamb from Auntie

Joyce. But nothing from her mum and dad.

Jodie looked at them, surprised. Then her dad winked at her mum. What was going on?

"Now open the cards!" he said.

Jodie tore open her cards. There were eight of them – the same number as her new age.

At the bottom of the pile was an ordinary-looking brown envelope with Jodie's name on it. "This doesn't look like a card," she said.

Mr Taylor peered at it. "It doesn't look like anything much."

"Looks like a bill," said Mrs Taylor, trying not to smile.

Jodie opened the envelope and

pulled out a small white square of paper. On it was written:

IOU one kitten.

Jodie looked at her mum and dad in astonishment. "What does this mean?"

"It means," said Mrs Taylor,

smiling, "that your dad and I owe you one birthday kitten – and we're going to collect it later."

Jodie gave a squeal of delight. "Really?" This was what she'd dreamed of for ages. But her mum and dad had always said no. Until now!

Mr Taylor did up his coat. "Mum's taking you to see a lady called Mrs Dent after school," he said. "She has a litter of kittens ready to go to new homes." He dropped a kiss on Jodie's head. "Got to rush. Have a lovely day!" And he left to go to work.

"A kitten," Jodie breathed. "A real live kitten." She gave her mum a hug.

Mrs Taylor smiled, then she

said, "Dad and I think you're old enough now to look after a pet of your own, Jodie."

"Oh, I am, I am!" Jodie said.

"So it's up to you to look after the kitten," Mrs Taylor went on. "You know how busy Dad and I are at the moment. We don't have time to feed and groom a pet or . . ." she pulled a face ". . . clear up any messes."

"Oh, there won't be any messes," Jodie said. She knew lots about pets and loved reading stories about cats. "Kittens are really clean. They're house-trained by their mothers from the moment they're born."

"I'm glad to hear it," said Mrs Taylor as she swished around the sink and gave it a little extra polish. "Because you know I can't bear any mess."

Jodie, used to her mum's neat and tidy ways, hardly heard her. She was getting a kitten! She was getting a kitten of her very own. She could hardly wait!

Chapter Two

"Oh, they're all lovely!" Jodie said, as five tiny kittens played about her feet. There were three fluffy grey kittens, like their mum, and two sweet black and white ones with pink noses.

Jodie sighed deeply. "I'm *never* going to be able to choose!" She got down on the floor and picked up each kitten in turn. "Oh, I don't know!" she wailed.

Jodie's mum smiled. "Can you help, Mrs Dent?"

"They're all good, clean little kittens," Mrs Dent said. "But the short-haired black and whites would be easier to care for. The grey kittens, being long-haired, will need lots more grooming."

"Oh, I won't mind doing that," Jodie said. "I shall love combing *my* kitten." She held up one of the grey fluffies. "This one has the bluest eyes. And he's *really* fluffy!"

The kitten looked at Jodie and miaowed. *Choose me!*

Jodie laughed and put him down so she could look at the

other kittens again. But she kept coming back to the fluffiest one.

The kitten went up to Jodie and rubbed his face against her ankle. "You look nice," he purred. "I'd miss my mum and my brothers and sisters – but I wouldn't mind coming home with you."

"I really think you'll have to

make up your mind, love,"
Jodie's mum said. "I'm sure Mrs
Dent has other things to do."

Jodie watched as the kittens
tumbled about, each trying to
look the sweetest.

"Come on, Jodie," said Mrs
Taylor.

The fluffiest kitten climbed onto
Jodie's trainer, mewing up at her.
And . . . well, if a kitten could
smile, he was doing it.

Jodie's heart melted. "OK, I
want . . ." She took a deep breath
then scooped up the fluffiest
kitten. "This one! I love him to
bits already."

Delighted, the kitten pushed his
head into Jodie's neck. "Good
choice," he purred.

"At last!" said Mrs Taylor.

"What are you going to call him, dear?" Mrs Dent asked, smiling.

Jodie thought hard. "I'm going to call him Felix," she said. She gave Felix a cuddle. "You're my fluffy Felix."

Tired from all his kitten capers, Felix closed his eyes, burrowed his nose into the crook of Jodie's arm and went to sleep.

Jodie's mum paid Mrs Dent, and Felix was put in the pet carrying box they'd bought from the local pet shop on the way.

Jodie looked down at her sleeping kitten and smiled. "Look," she said. "He's so fluffy that you can hardly tell which way round he is!"

"He does have a wonderful thick coat," Mrs Dent agreed. "The thickest I've ever seen. You'll need a special comb for grooming him. And he'll need combing every day." She wrote down the details for Jodie.

Jodie thanked her and gave Felix a gentle stroke before

closing the carrying box.

Still sleeping, Felix purred.
What a lovely life he was going to
have with his new family . . .

On the way home, Jodie and her
mum popped into Pearce's
Perfect Pets in the high street.

"Oh, you've brought your new
kitten in to see me," said Mr
Pearce, the owner.

Felix allowed himself to be lifted
out of his basket, put on the counter
and shown off to Mr Pearce.

"Well!" said Mr Pearce. "What a
fine kitten – and such a
wonderful coat."

Felix preened himself, purring
loudly. He could get used to all
this praise!

Jodie nodded, pleased. "He's lovely, isn't he?"

"You don't want to sell him, do you?" Mr Pearce joked.

"No way!" Jodie said. "We've come in to buy a special comb for grooming long-haired cats." She gave Mr Pearce the piece of paper Mrs Dent had given her, with the

type of comb written on it.

"I don't think I've got one in stock," said Mr Pearce. "But I'll order one for you. Jot down your phone number and I'll ring you when it's in."

"I hope it won't take long," Jodie's mum said, writing down their number. "I want that grey fluff combed out before it gets shed all over the house!"

Mr Pearce tickled Felix behind his ears. "With a thick coat like that, I reckon you'd soon comb enough fluff off him to knit yourself a woolly jumper!" he joked.

Jodie laughed. "I just want to keep him looking good."

"I tell you what," Mr Pearce

said. "He's such a handsome kitten that I'd like to take his photograph to put in my window. I'm sure it would attract a lot of attention. I'll give you the comb and a smart new collar in return. How's that?"

"Great!" said Jodie. "Can we, Mum?"

Mrs Taylor nodded. "I can't see why not," she said.

Felix began to wash around his face so that he'd look his best for the photograph.

"Why don't you choose a collar while I go and get my camera?" said Mr Pearce.

Jodie held a red and a green collar next to Felix, then chose the red one. She was carefully putting it on him when Mr Pearce came back with his camera.

Felix just loved attention. Everyone in the shop was watching him now. "How about this?" he purred, looking over his shoulder, his tail up straight. "Or this?" he miaowed, rolling on his back and looking up at the camera, his blue eyes wide. "Have you ever seen anything so sweet?"

"I think he knows he's being snapped," Mr Pearce said, grinning. "He's posing like a model. He thinks he's one of those supermodels."

Supermodel? Superkitten, more like, Felix thought.

Chapter Three

"You'll have to try to keep Felix off this sofa, Jodie," Mrs Taylor said a couple of days later.

Jodie had just come in from school and was sitting watching TV, with Felix on her lap.

Mrs Taylor dabbed at the sofa with a damp cloth, then frowned at the grey fluff she'd gathered up. "Dad sat down wearing his new suit and got it covered in grey hairs this morning," she went on.

"Sorry," Jodie said. "I'll try and brush some of the loose fluff out of Felix's coat later." She was going to make do with an old blue hairbrush until the special comb arrived at the pet shop.

Tutting a little under her breath, Mrs Taylor went over to the vacuum cleaner in the corner. "And this old vacuum cleaner of ours is hopeless!" she added.

"Shall I have a go with it?" Jodie offered, feeling guilty at the extra work Felix's fluff was making for her mum.

Mrs Taylor shook her head. "It's much too heavy for you to lug around, love. It's too heavy for me, come to that!" She plugged in the big old machine and switched it on.

Felix, who'd been snoozing, sat bolt upright. *What* was that horrible roaring noise? He jumped down and made a dash for the stairs. Pale grey fluff hung in the air as he ran . . .

It was Saturday and Jodie was taking her time in the bathroom. She didn't have to rush to school this morning and could play with her new kitten all day.

Felix had decided to keep Jodie company while she showered,

and was perched on the edge of the bath. He bobbed from side to side, dabbing his paw in the drops of water. "Why can't I catch these little round silvery things?" he miaowed sharply. It was very annoying!

Jodie turned off the shower and put a dollop of soapy foam on the edge of the bath for Felix to play with.

Felix looked at the white froth. He reached out a paw – but the bit he touched seemed to disappear. Very odd.

He leaned over to sniff the strange stuff – and jumped back in surprise, sneezing as tiny soapy bubbles flew up his nose. Felix lost his balance and slid into

the bath, a wisp of foam still on
his nose.

"Oh, Felix!" Jodie cried. "You
silly puss!"

Jodie couldn't stop laughing as
she lifted Felix out of the bath.

Then she noticed the hairs that
had flown off Felix as he'd
skidded into the bath. She
grabbed a cloth and quickly

wiped them up before her mum noticed. Jodie could hear the vacuum cleaner on again, downstairs.

Felix had been with the Taylors for just over a week now, and he had settled in really well. But there was one big problem: his fluff!

Felix's lovely thick coat shed oodles of fluffy hair wherever Felix went. And Mrs Taylor was *not* pleased about it.

Jodie got dressed and took Felix into her bedroom. "Time to brush out some of that fluff," she said to him, setting him down on her bed.

She went to find the old blue hairbrush. But when she came

back, Felix had vanished. Then
she noticed a fluffy tail, fat as a
squirrel's, sticking out of the
duvet. "I can see you!" she called.

Jodie flung back the duvet to
find Felix crouched down ready
to pounce. He leapt into the air,
scrabbled up her back and landed
on her shoulder. "You're back!

Let's play!" he miaowed loudly.

As Jodie collapsed onto the bed, giggling, her mum appeared in the doorway.

"Just look at all that fluff on your bedclothes, Jodie," Mrs Taylor said frowning. "You'd better change them. And don't you think it's about time you started grooming that kitten? If you combed out all that loose fluff it wouldn't come out all over the house!"

"I'm going to, Mum – right now," Jodie said, and held up the brush to show her.

With a sigh, Mrs Taylor went back to her cleaning. Pulling Felix onto her lap, Jodie gently began to stroke the brush along his back.

But as far as Felix was concerned, the bristly blue creature was trying to attack him! He sprang round. "How dare you!" he hissed, ready to fight the brush.

Jodie sighed. "Come on, Felix, you have to let me groom you – otherwise we'll *both* be in trouble!"

Just then, the vacuum cleaner stopped again, and Mrs Taylor called from the bathroom. "Jodie, leave that kitten alone for a moment and come in here, will you?"

Jodie put the brush down on the bed and went out to her mum. Felix pounced on the blue creature, biting and kicking it.

"Caught you!" he growled happily.

"Have you had Felix in here with you?" Jodie's mum asked sternly when Jodie went into the bathroom.

Jodie nodded. "He likes to sit and watch me clean my teeth."

"I thought so," Mrs Taylor said, "because there are hairs in the sink *and* on the flannels." Mrs Taylor shook her head. "Wherever I look there's a smudge of grey fluff!"

"But what can I do, Mum?" Jodie said. "Felix can't help moulting."

"I never seem to stop cleaning these days," Mrs Taylor

grumbled. "Not since Felix arrived." And then she stared at a toothbrush in horror. "That's the limit!" she cried. "There's cat hair on my toothbrush!"

"Perhaps the special comb we've ordered from the pet shop will work," Jodie said.

Her mum nodded. "I hope so – I feel quite worn out with all the extra work."

Feeling guilty, Jodie escaped back to her bedroom and watched as Felix burrowed under her duvet again, leaving a cloud of grey fluff behind him. She just hoped that Felix would allow her to use the new comb on him. If he didn't, she could see things getting *very* difficult . . .

Chapter Four

A couple of days later, Jodie and her mum made their way to Pearce's Perfect Pets after school. Mr Pearce had called to say the special comb was in.

As they approached the pet shop Jodie noticed that Felix's photograph was now in the window. "Oh, look, Mum!" she pointed. "There's Felix! Doesn't he look gorgeous?"

They both stopped and stared at the big photograph of Felix in the middle of the window display. He was wearing his new collar, with his head on one side, looking his cutest. A slogan above the picture read:

POSH PETS COME TO
PEARCE'S

Mrs Taylor nodded. "Yes, he looks lovely." Then she gave a little sigh. "But sometimes I can't help wishing that you'd chosen one of the short-haired kittens."

"Don't say that, Mum!" Jodie

protested. "I love Felix. He's the most beautiful kitten in the world!"

"He's certainly the fluffiest!" said Mrs Taylor. And then she smiled. "He *is* gorgeous, and I'm awfully fond of him. But he makes such a lot of mess!"

As they went into the shop, Jodie looked once more at the

beautiful photograph of Felix. Who would have thought that choosing the fluffiest kitten would cause such a lot of problems?

"I *wish* you'd let me comb you, Felix!" Jodie said. "It might help with all the fluff, you know."

"Purreow!" Felix said. "I've decided I don't like those things called brushes and combs – they mess up my lovely fur."

Jodie had tried the special comb for long-haired cats for the first time yesterday. But it hadn't been a great success. Felix treated it just like the blue hairbrush.

As he rolled on the carpet, showing his soft fluffy tummy,

Jodie put her hand out for the comb. Half-hiding it in her hand, she very gently combed down his tummy with it and collected some soft fluff in its plastic teeth.

Felix sprang to life. *That* thing again! "Miaow!" He jumped on it, caught it and gave it a good old bite.

"Oh, *Felix*!" Jodie cried, pulling the comb away from him. It already had tiny teeth marks in the handle, where Felix had attacked it yesterday. His kitten teeth were sharp as needles.

"Oh, don't you want to play, then?" Felix miaowed.

Jodie sighed as she heard the monster cleaner roaring away downstairs again. "Maybe you'll let me groom you when you get older," she said.

Felix stared up at her with his bright blue eyes. No, he didn't think so . . .

Just then, the doorbell rang downstairs and the vacuum cleaner was hastily switched off. As Mrs Taylor opened the door,

Jodie could hear a very familiar voice. Then her mum called upstairs.

"Jodie! Mrs Oberon's here. Come and say hello!"

Jodie gathered Felix up. "Mrs Oberon is organising the school fête this year," she told him. "She's my teacher. She's a bit posh and strict – but quite nice really."

"Of course I'd be delighted to help at the school fête," Mrs Taylor was saying, as Jodie carried Felix into the sitting room. "Just let me know what you'd like me to do."

The smartly-dressed visitor was sitting on the sofa. "Oh thank you!" she said. Then she smiled at Jodie. "Hello, Jodie – lovely kitten!" she added, seeing Felix. "Maybe we should have a cat competition at the fête. He'd be bound to win!"

Felix purred with pleasure. He liked Mrs Oberon.

Jodie and her mum showed Mrs Oberon to the door, then waited until their guest had reached the front gate.

Suddenly, Mrs Taylor gasped. "Oh no!"

"What?" Jodie asked, puzzled.

"Mrs Oberon's skirt!" Mrs Taylor whispered.

"What about it?" Jodie asked, even more puzzled. She hadn't noticed anything strange about it.

"Didn't you see?" said her

mum, closing the door. "All down the back of it – grey fluff!"

Jodie went into the sitting room to look at the sofa. There was fluff all over the cushions again. She hurriedly tried to brush it off.

"I thought I told you not to let that kitten on the sofa!" Mrs Taylor thundered.

Felix, who was still sitting on the sofa, took one look at Mrs Taylor's angry face and disappeared underneath it.

"This is so embarrassing!" Jodie's mum went on. "What on earth will Mrs Oberon think when she gets home and sees her skirt covered in fluff?" Jodie didn't really think there was anything wrong with having cat

fluff on your skirt. Or on the
carpet or the sofa, or in the bath.
But her mum sighed heavily.
"This is the last straw! I'm
beginning to think that kitten of
yours ought to live in the garage,
you know."

"Mum!" Jodie protested. "We
can't do that – he'd hate it!"

Felix, lying flat underneath the sofa, gave a frightened squeak. This was going too far! A kitten – a *super*kitten like him – couldn't possibly live in a *garage*.

"Well, I just can't think of another solution," Mrs Taylor said. "He refuses to be groomed, he won't stay off the furniture . . . and all I do is clean the place morning, noon and night!"

"But, Mum—" Jodie was just about to start pleading with her mum when the phone rang.

"Bill Pearce here, lass," a voice said when Jodie answered it. "From Pearce's Perfect Pets. How's your fluffy kitten?"

"Er . . . he's OK," Jodie said, looking at her mum, who was

still frowning and was about to start vacuuming again.

"And did the new comb do the trick?" Mr Pearce asked.

"Not exactly," Jodie said uncomfortably.

"Well, it's about that – about the fluff – that I'm ringing you," Mr Pearce went on. "Can I have a word with your mum?"

Jodie handed the phone to Mrs Taylor, who spoke with Mr Pearce for a while.

Then she put the phone down, looking puzzled. "Mr Pearce says that he has some people in his shop who want to meet Felix," she said.

Hearing his name, Felix gave a mew of alarm and crawled to the

very back of the sofa. What was
happening *now*?

"What's it about, Mum?" Jodie
asked, surprised.

"He wouldn't say," Mrs Taylor
replied. "But they're coming
round straight away." She
switched on the vacuum cleaner.
"It all sounds most mysterious."

Chapter Five

"Hello," Jodie said shyly, as Mr Pearce brought a small, smiling man and a tall woman with frizzy red hair into the house.

"This is Mr Tomkins and his assistant, Miss Spark," said Mr Pearce.

"Pleased to meet you," said

Jodie's mum, shaking hands with them. "Although I can't think why you wanted to meet Felix."

Felix was watching from underneath the sofa. What did these people want with him?

"If I may explain," Mr Tomkins said, stepping forward. "My assistant, Miss Spark here, visited Mr Pearce's shop a few days ago and admired the photograph of Felix in the window . . ."

Felix, with a soft miaow, came out from under the sofa. "Here I am!"

The two visitors gave an "*Aaah*!" of admiration.

"Oh, how sweet!" Miss Spark cried. Her red curls bobbed round her pointy face. "Mr Pearce told me that Felix was the fluffiest kitten he'd ever seen!" she said.

"And I'm pleased to see he's very fluffy indeed," Mr Tomkins added.

Jodie picked up Felix and stroked him proudly. A small shower of grey fluff floated out from his coat. Everyone watched as it slowly sank to the floor. Jodie's heart sank too. Was her mum going to be angry?

"Ahem . . ." said Miss Spark. "Mr Pearce also told me you were having a spot of trouble with Felix's fluff."

"Well, yes," said Mrs Taylor. She glanced at Jodie. "It's true that all I seem to do these days is clean up after Felix. I've got a vacuum

cleaner but it's not really up to the job."

"And that is why we're here!" boomed Mr Tomkins happily.

"Shall I go and get it, sir?" Miss Spark asked, a hint of excitement in her voice.

Mr Tomkins nodded. "If you don't mind, Miss Spark."

Miss Spark went to the white van parked outside. She came back in carrying a strange, shiny machine. Written on the side, in bright blue letters, was *Wizard*.

"It looks like a robot!" Jodie said, staring at the large silver box with arms attached.

Felix jumped down from Jodie's arms and approached the machine. What a strange-looking creature! He saw himself in the shiny surface. "Miiaoww!" What a fine-looking kitten!

"This," said Mr Tomkins proudly, "is my latest invention. It's not *just* a vacuum cleaner..."

Felix backed away from the silver creature. "Is *that* a vacuum cleaner?" he miaowed.

". . . It's *the* vacuum cleaner!"
Mr Tomkins continued. "Better
than any other!" He beamed at
Jodie and her mum. "I've called it
the Wizard because it can clean
any house like magic!"

"Really?" Mrs Taylor looked at
it wistfully. "Well, it looks very
good, but—"

Mr Tomkins held up his
hand. "Please allow us to
demonstrate . . ." He turned to his
assistant. "Miss Spark, would you
plug in the Wizard, please?"

"Certainly, Mr Tomkins," his
assistant replied. By now, Miss
Spark's red curls seemed to fizz
with excitement.

Felix wondered if he should
make a dash for it. He'd heard

the dreaded words "vacuum cleaner", and that usually meant trouble.

But while he was deciding, Miss Spark switched the machine on. The silver creature began to hum.

Felix sat with his head on one side and stared, puzzled. Why wasn't it making a nasty loud roaring sound like Mrs Taylor's vacuum cleaner?

Miss Spark began to put the machine through its paces, moving one of its long rubbery arms over the sofa.

"Look at that!" Mrs Taylor cried, delighted. The sofa cushions looked brand new!

Then Miss Spark pushed the machine across the carpet. "With

one gentle push, the Wizard slides easily along the floor, picking up every single hair as it passes," she said.

"It picks up fluff you didn't know you had!" Mr Tomkins joked.

Felix watched the humming silver creature gliding smoothly along the carpet. It didn't seem fierce, like the other vacuum cleaner. And he did like being able to see himself in the creature's shiny body. Perhaps he should make friends with it.

Felix ran towards the machine, jumped on it and pawed at his reflection.

"Felix looks as if he's driving it!" Jodie laughed.

Everyone smiled, watching Felix as he sat on the Wizard like a figurehead. His purring was almost as loud as the Wizard's hum.

As Miss Spark steered the Wizard past Jodie, Felix looked up. "Hey, Jodie!" he miaowed. "This is fun!"

Mrs Taylor shook her head in awe, looking at the spotless sofa and carpet. "I've never seen the place looking so clean," she said. "At least, not since Felix has been here."

Jodie had to agree.

"And finally," said Miss Spark as she switched the vacuum cleaner off, "the Wizard also sucks fluff and dust from the air – before it has a chance to settle."

"That's fantastic!" Jodie said.

As the machine stopped moving, Felix stepped off and sat next to his new friend, his head on one side.

Mr Pearce began clapping. "It looks as though Felix thinks he's done the cleaning himself," he said.

"He's an absolute darling!" Miss Spark cried.

Felix was really enjoying himself. Everyone seemed to think he was great! And now that his silver friend had cleaned up all his fluff, perhaps Mrs Taylor would forget about banishing him to the garage.

But Jodie's mum was looking worried again. "It's a marvellous machine," she said. "I'd love one – but I'm afraid we simply can't afford a new vacuum cleaner. Especially such an expensive-looking one . . ."

"Oh, I don't want you to *buy* one!" Mr Tomkins said.

Chapter Six

"What?" Mrs Taylor said in surprise.

"Let me explain," said Mr Tomkins. "We want Felix to star in our advertisements," he said.

Jodie gasped.

"He's a natural," Mr Tomkins went on. "With Felix showing off the Wizard, we'll sell thousands!"

"Oh, wow!" Jodie cried. She picked up Felix and hugged him. "You're going to be famous!" she whispered.

Felix rubbed his head against Jodie's neck. "Great!" he purred. "I've always wanted to be a superkitten."

"I can see the posters now," Mr Tomkins said, rubbing his hands together happily. "They'll say: *Buy a Wizard – the ultimate fluffbuster!*"

"Or how about: *So quiet it won't even frighten a kitten!*" Miss Spark added.

"Very good, Miss Spark!" Mr Tomkins boomed.

"And: *So light even a kitten can*

push it!" Mr Pearce offered. "If you don't mind me joining in," he added, going a bit red.

"Thank you, Mr Pearce! Another excellent suggestion!" cried Mr Tomkins. Then he turned to Jodie's mum. "We'll pay a fee, of course. And the 'Wizard Kitten' must have a Wizard for his own home. We'll leave this one for you, shall we?"

Jodie and her mum stood there, too astounded to speak. Felix gave a short miaow. "Say yes!" He wanted to be a superkitten. He wanted to be famous – and he wanted it now!

One evening, a few weeks later, Jodie and her mum and dad were

all sitting in front of the
television. Felix was sitting on
Jodie's lap. He was quite a bit
bigger, but still very fluffy.

"Mr Tomkins said it would be
on at five-thirty," Jodie said. She
looked at her watch. "It's nearly
that now."

"I only make it twenty-five

past," Mr Taylor said.

Felix looked up at Jodie, his bright blue eyes puzzled. Why was everyone so excited? Even Jodie's dad had come home from work early.

"Have we got the video set?" Mrs Taylor asked.

Just then there was a noise outside in the hall and a cheerful woman put her head around the door. It was Mrs Bell.

Felix turned round and miaowed. "Hello, Mrs Bell." He liked Mrs Bell. Ever since Mr Tomkins had paid a lot of money for Felix's kitten modelling, Mrs Bell had been coming here to do all the cleaning.

"I've finished cleaning

upstairs," Mrs Bell said. "Do you want me to do in here now?"

"Oh, Mrs Bell," said Jodie's mum, smiling. "Come and watch the advertisement first! It should be on any min—"

She was interrupted by a scream from Jodie. "Here he is! Oh, look, Felix, there you are!"

Jodie held Felix up in front of the television and he saw himself sitting proudly on a Wizard as it was put through its paces.

"*Solve even the fluffiest problem with the aid of your* Wizard!" said a voice on the TV. "*Cleans your home like magic!*"

"Don't you look gorgeous!" Jodie cried.

"Purreow!" said Felix. He

jumped down and sat as close to the TV as he could, staring up at himself. "Yes, I do look pretty good . . ."

As the advertisement ended, everyone sighed with pride. Then Felix gave a tiny sneeze and shook himself, sending a shower of fluffy grey fur into the air.

Jodie laughed. "You can do that as much as you like, Felix," she said. "Because now you're getting paid for it!"